MW00803042

NOTES

From Lee

Our son Riff will ask, "Dad, tell me one of your stories." When I tell him stories, I make them up on the spot.
It's a creative exercise for me and a creative example for him. Normally I forget them afterwards but this particular story
stuck with me. I wrote it down that night. A week later I structured and printed it out. I presented it to my wife and said,
"Babe, you gotta draw this with your secret skills!" Then one day out of the blue, the spirit moved her and she didn't stop
until the entire book was finished. She drew right on the pages I printed out. We scanned them in, called our good friend
and graphic designer, Jerome Curchod to put the polish on, and he prepped the book in your hands.

From Scarlett

When our son was around three, he started requesting drawings of specific characters he wanted to play with.
I'd draw a Pokémon, a Smurf, an Angry Bird, (or whatever his favorite was at the time), color it, and cut it out.
Riff would create worlds with these "paper dolls" and play for hours. I must've created over a hundred of them.
Little did I realize this would open up a love for illustrating, and these characters would lead to creating our own originals.
I didn't stray from the formula. I used the tools in our craft cubby. Mostly crayons, pencils, and sharpies.

From Riff

Man, this book is really fun. I think kids my age (8) or younger would enjoy this fabulous book created by The Cherry Family!

We love this book. Obviously because of the story and illustrations, but most importantly
because it's an original, collaborative, family creation.

We hope you enjoy our story!

Lots of Love from the Cherry's

MANY YEARS LATER, JACK AND BILLY BOB CAME BACK TO THE LEGENDARY MUSIC TREE. THIS TIME THEY CAME WITH A DEVICE THAT RECORDS AND PLAYS BACK SOUNDS.

THEY SAT DOWN, SET UP THEIR RECORDER AND WAITED FOR THE WIND TO BLOW.

BILLY BOB FELT THE ENTIRE TOWN LOOKING AT HIM.
SOME SOBBING, SOME CHEERING, AND SOME WITH A LOOK OF KNOWING
BECAUSE THE TREE HAD HEALED OR HELPED THEM IN SOME WAY.

BILLY BOB FELT THE MAGIC OF THE LEGENDARY MUSIC TREE SO DEEPLY,
HE THOUGHT HE WAS ACTUALLY HEARING THE MUSIC.

IT VIBRATED DEEP WITHIN ITS WOODEN SOUL.

SOME WOULD EVEN SAY BILLY BOB'S AXE CHOPS IMPROVED THE SOUND.

CREATING THE MOST MAGICAL, BEAUTIFUL MUSIC ANYONE HAS EVER HEARD.

THE BREEZE PICKED UP AND BLEW A GIANT GUST OF WIND...

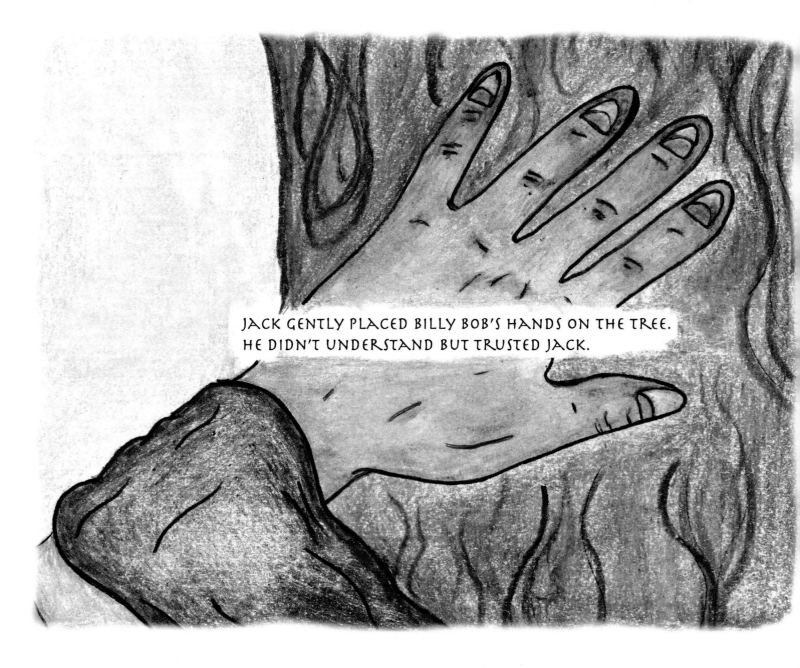

BILLY BOB MOUTHED TO JACK SINCE HE COULDN'T SPEAK THAT WELL.

THE TOWNSPEOPLE RAN BACK TO THE SCENE.

NO REWARD WAS WORTH DESTROYING SOMETHING SO UNIQUE AND BEAUTIFUL.

IT STOPPED HIM COLD.

JACK HAD EVER HEARD IN HIS LIFE.

PEOPLE CAME FROM ALL AROUND TO SEE AND HEAR IT.

IT WAS SHAPED SO PERFECTLY, IT MADE MUSIC WHENEVER THE WIND BLEW.

THE LEGENDARY MUSIC TREE

Written by Lee Cherry
Illustrated by Scarlett Cherry
Inspired by Riff Cherry